Super Soren

the magical adventures of an underdog

written by kristen perhach

illustrated by margarita fomenko

Published by Super Soren Inc. 2017

Super Soren Inc.
Attention: Kristen Perhach
Kristen@supersoren.com

Information about Illustrations:
All gorgeous illustrations were created by Margarita Fomenko, in a Work-For-Hire arrangement, for Super Soren Inc.
Want to contact Margarita? Email mfomenko.art@gmail.com

Ordering information: Special discounts are available on quantity purchases by corporations, associations, and others. For details, contact Kristen at the email address above.

ISBN Information
Hardcover: 978-0-578-52860-1
Digital: 978-0-578-53971-3

Library of Congress number: 2019909121

To Steve, Soren, and Fitz ~ my loves, my life, my heart
For Ann Marie and Sarah Jane
For girls and boys everywhere ~ may you always
feel your courage and power
~ Kristen

To Roman ~ my soul, my best friend and love
For all children ~ dream wide and be brave
Life is full of magical moments
~ Margarita

Soren often played by herself.

She imagined she was swimming underwater with dolphins,
whales and shiny fish of all sizes, shapes and colors. She liked
to collect rocks, do science experiments and math puzzles.

Soren was a little different. Girls at school called her weird,
especially Marcy. Even though Soren liked being by herself,
she wished that the other girls would be kinder to her.

Was it her freckles? Her glasses? Her green eyes?
She couldn't understand why she didn't fit in.

One day at recess, Soren was on the soccer field, spinning
around and around, imagining she was inside a tornado!
She stopped when she got too dizzy.

Wobbling a little, she saw a group of girls pointing and
laughing at her.

"Why do you do such weird things?" Marcy called with a sneer.
"No one likes you."

Soren felt as small as a mouse. She said nothing and looked
down at her feet. A tear rolled down her hot cheek.

How could someone say such mean things?
Soren sat down, feeling sad and lonely.

That night Soren told Mom and Dad what had happened.

"Try not to be too sad," said Dad. "You're perfect as you are, and you shouldn't try to change to fit in."

Soren's little sister Sarah Jane gave her a hug.

Tomorrow was Saturday. Soren was glad she'd be able to do lots of playing. She dreamt of the fun she'd have spending the day at her fort in the forest behind her house.

The next morning, Soren walked along the forest path while playing with her little dog Ruffles.

When they reached the fort, Soren sat down to write and draw in her Book of Dreams – a place for her secrets and deepest thoughts.

Then, she focused on her fort. Soren made her fort's roof stronger by putting big and small branches on it. Ruffles helped too.

As the sun sank lower in the sky, Soren and Ruffles set off for home.

Next to the path was a large old tree that Soren had seen many times before.

But as she passed the tree, something caught her eye. It looked like...could it be...?

Soren thought she saw a tiny face peeking around the tree trunk, but then it was gone.

She shook her head. She must have been seeing things!

Soren went over for a closer look. Around the side of the tree trunk was a tiny door!

"I wonder where it leads to?" Soren said to Ruffles.

The door was painted a shiny red, and there was a gleaming, golden doorknob. Soren gently turned the knob and opened the door.

Inside was a tiny bed, a chair and table, and a little fireplace with a pot hanging over it. There were small bottles of all sizes. Many were filled with brightly colored liquids. Others had sparkly golden dust.

"Are these Magic potions?" Soren wondered aloud to Ruffles.
Soren quickly realized that whoever lived there must be very small!
"Hello!" she called out. "Is anyone here?"

There was a rustling noise in a nearby bush. Soren spun around to see
a tiny person dressed all in purple, with a pointy yellow hat!
Soren couldn't believe her eyes!

She quickly exclaimed, "Who are you?"
But in a flash, the little person disappeared into thin air,
leaving behind only a few spots of shimmery dust.

Soren noticed something on the ground. It was a scroll tied with a shiny, dark-blue ribbon. She opened it quickly.

Soren was shocked to see it was a letter for her! She noticed a drawing of a five-point star with two S's connected at the bottom of the page.

The moment Soren finished reading, the wind spiraled leaves up and around her. This was surely a sign. She didn't know who sent the letter, but she felt it was right.

She put her hands on her heart and felt it beating. Soren knew that she had the power, strength and courage within her after all.

"Super Soren," she whispered. Then, with more force she shouted, "Super Soren!"

She ran home with Ruffles and showed Mom, Dad and Sarah Jane the letter. "I think that this star is a symbol for you - Super Soren!" Mom exclaimed with pride.

The next morning, Mom had a surprise for Soren. "I made something for you," she said. It was a beautiful cape with the Super Soren star on it!

"Now you can look and feel as brave as you truly are. Remember, even when you're not wearing it, you still have strength and courage."

Soren put on the cape and set off with Ruffles to her forest fort.
"I am brave! I am strong! I am Super Soren!" she said as she played.
"Woof!" agreed Ruffles.

On her way home, Soren suddenly remembered the little red door.

She ran lightning quick yelling, "Super Soren!"

Slowly, she opened the bright red door. This time there was nothing inside. Soren felt especially disappointed.

She put her hand in and touched the floor. It felt sandy.

When she took it out, she was surprised to see it was covered in glittering golden dust.

"What's this?" Soren asked. She blew it off her hand and watched it scatter into the air.

She heard a faint laugh. Out of the corner of her eye saw she the tiny person! But once again, they vanished.

"Wait! Who are you?!"

There was no answer. She sat for a minute hoping they'd return. After some time, Soren ran home yelling, "Suuuuuuper Sooooren!" all along the way.

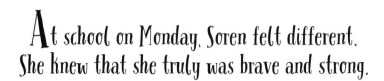At school on Monday, Soren felt different.
She knew that she truly was brave and strong.

At recess, Soren looked for rocks to add to her collection. As she bent down
to pick up a shiny, clear stone, a shadow fell over her. It was Marcy.

"Hey everyone, look!" Marcy called. "Soren's playing with a rock!"

Soren's heart beat swiftly. Her heart - that was where her courage
came from! She took a deep breath and looked Marcy in the eye.

"You won't be mean to me anymore, Marcy!" she said. "Stop it right now."

Marcy opened and shut her mouth, but didn't say a word.
Quickly, she walked away.

Soren felt proud of herself. "Super Soren," she whispered.

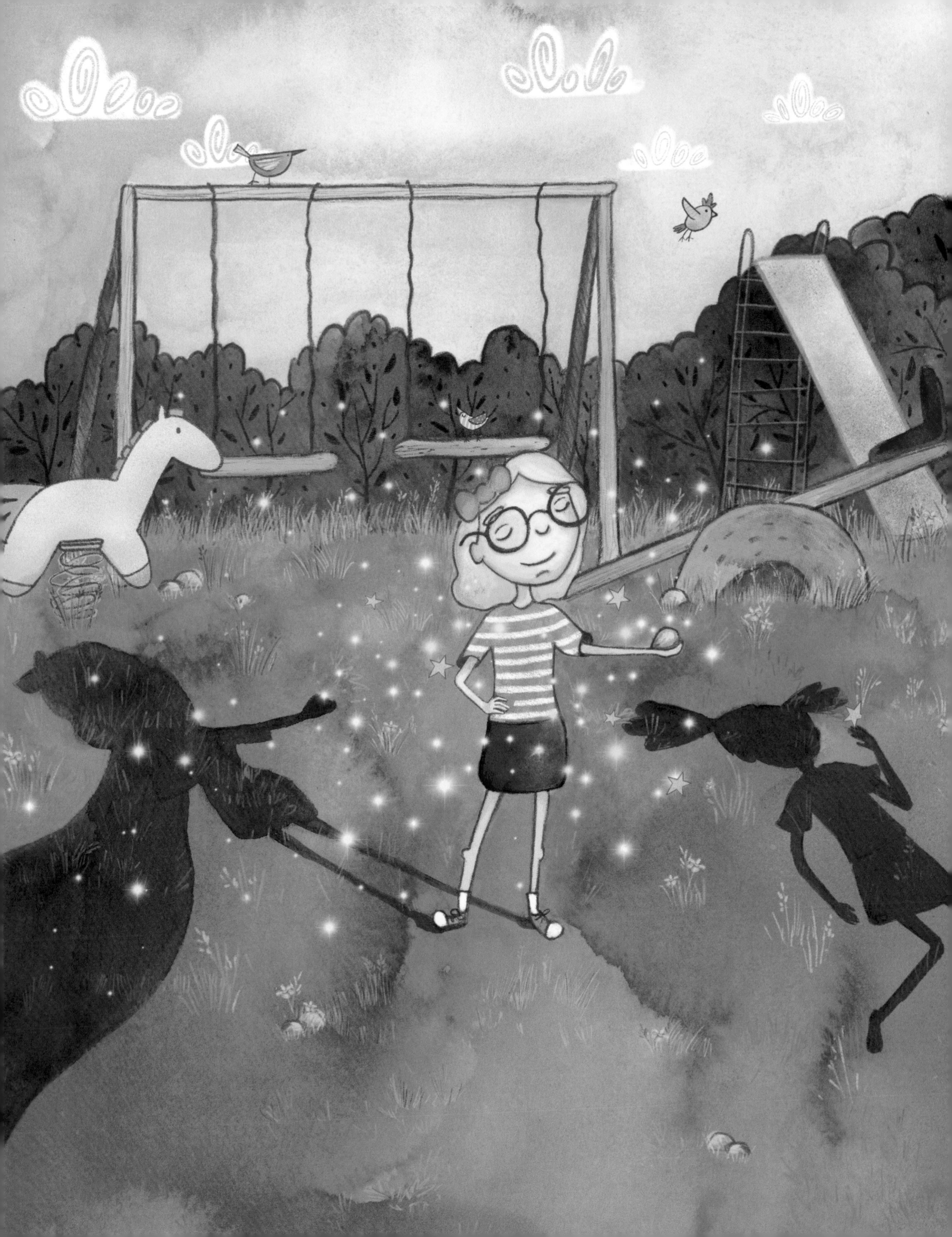

At bedtime that night, Soren noticed something on her pillow. It was another beautiful scroll. Scattered around it was golden, shimmery dust.

The note read, "Super Soren, we are so proud of you. Keep being strong and brave." Soren knew that she would.

"Hmmm," she thought. "Tomorrow I'll go back to the little door in the forest. Maybe there will be something new there, just for me..."